Five reasons why you'll love Isadora Moon...

Meet the magical,
fang-tastic Isadora Moon!

Isadora's cuddly toy, Pink Rabbit,
has been magicked to life!

There's a new girl
in Isadora's class!

Isadora is having
a teddy bears' picnic.

Enchanting
pink and black
pictures!

If a new person started at your school, how would you make them feel welcome?

I would make them a huge card and get them a cupcake. - Lyla, age 8

I'd ask if they wanted to play me with at break time and they could pick the game! - Edie, age 6

I would invite them over for a playdate to get to know them better. - Zahavah, age 9

I would welcome them with a big friendly smile every day. - Thandie, age 7

I would teach them to do good things and not *whispers* 'guys, let's pour a bucket of water over the teacher's head'. - Holly, age 7

I would treat them like how I would want to be treated, which would be to feel included. - Genevieve, age almost 8

Family Tree

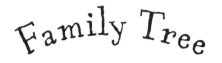

My Mum
Countess Cordelia
Moon

Baby Honeyblossom

My Dad
Count Bartholomew
Moon

Pink Rabbit

Me!
Isadora Moon

For vampires, fairies, and humans everywhere!
And for my sparkly Celestine.

Illustrated by Mike Garton,
based on original artwork by Harriet Muncaster

OXFORD
UNIVERSITY PRESS

Great Clarendon Street, Oxford OX2 6DP
Oxford University Press is a department of the University of Oxford.
It furthers the University's objective of excellence in research, scholarship,
and education by publishing worldwide. Oxford is a registered trade mark
of Oxford University Press in the UK and in certain other countries

Copyright © Harriet Muncaster 2023

The moral rights of the author have been asserted

Database right Oxford University Press (maker)

First published in 2023

British Library Cataloguing in Publication Data

Data available

ISBN:978-0-19-277808-6

1 3 5 7 9 10 8 6 4 2

Printed in Great Britain by Bell and Bain Ltd, Glasgow

The manufacturing process conforms to the environmental
regulations of the country of origin.

MIX
Paper | Supporting
responsible forestry
FSC
www.fsc.org   **FSC® C007785**

ISADORA ✦ MOON

and the New Girl

Harriet Muncaster

OXFORD
UNIVERSITY PRESS

Chapter ONE

It was the first day of a new term and
when I arrived at school I was surprised to
see a new girl standing at the front of the
classroom.

'This is Ava,' said Miss Cherry. 'She's
new in town and she'll be joining our class
from today. Let's all welcome her!'

'Welcome, Ava!' chanted the class.

I watched as Miss Cherry led Ava to an empty desk at the back of the room and remembered how it had felt to be new in the class myself. It had been a bit scary!

I wondered if Ava felt scared too. She wasn't smiling and she kept reaching her hand up to her dress pocket.

At break time everyone in the class swarmed over to Ava in the playground. We were all interested in getting to know her.

'I *really* like your shoes, Ava!' I said, pointing at them.

'Me too!' said my best friend Zoe.

Ava was wearing a pair of super sparkly lace-up boots with silver stars. I wasn't sure if she was really supposed to be wearing them at school, but I wondered if Miss Cherry hadn't said anything because she was new.

Ava looked at me and Zoe, but she didn't smile or say thank you.

'They're nice, aren't they,' she said, sticking out her foot so that the glitter dazzled in the sunlight. 'Much better than any of your boring old school shoes!'

I heard Zoe gasp next to me and I stared in shock at Ava, but Bruno laughed. He didn't care that Ava thought his shoes were boring.

'Where have you moved from?' he asked. 'Was it from far away?'

'Far enough away to have to move schools,' said Ava and she sounded a bit cross. 'I was at a *much* better school before this. It had a *swimming pool*! And my friends there were *fabulous*!' She glared round at us all and I suddenly felt completely small and very *un*-fabulous.

'Oh, right,' said Bruno. He shrugged and then went off to play football with Jasper and Sashi.

Zoe and I stayed where we were but I wasn't sure what else to say to Ava.

'Do you want to come and play with us?' asked Zoe after a moment. 'We're going to make a crown for Pink Rabbit from daisies!'

Pink Rabbit bounced up and down beside me with excitement. He used to be my favourite stuffed toy, but my mum magicked him alive with her wand. She can do things like that because she's a fairy.

Ava frowned. Then she glanced scornfully at Pink Rabbit and said, 'Aren't you a bit old to be bringing a cuddly toy to school?'

I stared at Ava, speechless. Tears started to prick at the corners of my eyes. Pink Rabbit stopped bouncing and glared indignantly at the new girl. Zoe took my hand.

'Well!' she blustered. 'That's fine. We'll go and play on our own then!'

'Good,' said Ava, defiantly. 'I have better things to do.' Then she marched across to the other side of the playground, sat down on a bench and opened a notebook.

Zoe pulled me by the hand over to the school playing field. It was dotted all over with daisies, but neither of us could concentrate on making a crown for Pink Rabbit.

'I can't believe how horrible Ava is!' Zoe huffed. 'I've never met such a mean girl before!'

'Me neither!' I said. And it was true. Ava was *mean*. None of my friends from school had ever spoken to me like that before. I picked up Pink Rabbit and gave him a big squeeze, trying to stop any tears from falling from my eyes.

'Just ignore her, Isadora,' said Zoe. 'She's probably just jealous that she doesn't have a Pink Rabbit. I'll bring in my toy monkey tomorrow!'

'OK,' I sniffed. Then I looked at Zoe and smiled. I felt so glad to have a best friend like her!

'How was school?' asked Mum when I got home that afternoon.

'It was all right,' I shrugged. 'There's a new girl called Ava. But she wasn't very nice.'

'Oh?' said Mum. 'Why not?'

'She just wasn't,' I said.

'OK . . .' said Mum. She set a plate down in front of me. On it was a peanut butter sandwich, which is my favourite snack, but today it didn't taste quite as good as usual.

'I'm sure Ava will warm up,' said Mum as she sat down opposite me and started to feed my baby sister Honeyblossom some pink milk. 'It's

probably just because she's new.'

'Maybe,' I said, but inside I was sure that Ava would never warm up. I wished that she had never joined our class!

'Shall we talk about something more cheering?' suggested Dad as he slurped his red juice. My dad is a vampire and he only likes food if it's red. 'Why don't we discuss Pink Rabbit's party!'

'Oh yes!' I said, immediately feeling a lot better. I had been begging Mum and Dad to let me hold a party for Pink Rabbit for ages. He's never had one!

'I want to invite all my friends over with their favourite toys for a picnic in the garden!' I said.

13

'That sounds lovely,' said Mum. 'I'll make a cake!'

'A teddy bears' picnic!' said Dad. 'Pink Rabbit will love it!'

Pink Rabbit wiggled his ears in agreement.

'*Maybe* we could have a bouncy castle too?' I said hopefully.

'We'll see,' replied Mum. 'Are you going to invite the new girl?'

I felt all my excitement about the party suddenly drain right out of me.

'No,' I replied. 'She'll only ruin it.'

Mum frowned.

'I really think you should,' she said.

'But . . .' I mumbled. 'I don't want to. And anyway, I'm sure she wouldn't *want* to come. She'd think a teddy bears' picnic was babyish.'

'I'm sure she wouldn't!' said Dad. 'And besides, you'll be busy hosting so you won't have to spend that much time with her at the party if you don't want to. It would be very unkind to leave her out.'

'Yes,' agreed Mum. 'Think about how you felt when you were new at school.'

'*I* was nice when I was new!' I said indignantly. 'I didn't tell people they had boring shoes or that they were babyish for having a cuddly toy!'

'Is that what she said?' Dad gasped. He stuck out his foot in its shiny, polished vampire shoe. 'Well! If someone ever dared to insult *my* footwear—'

Mum gave him a sharp look.

'*Ahem,*' said Dad. 'I'm sure the new girl didn't mean it.'

'She did!' I insisted.

'Even if she did,' said Mum, 'and *even* if she isn't very nice, you really can't leave

her out if you're inviting everyone else in your class. I'm sorry, Isadora.'

I gave a long sigh, but deep down I knew Mum was right.

'*Ohh . . . kaay,*' I said. 'I'll invite Ava.'

'Good,' smiled Mum. 'It's the right thing to do.'

'Just give her a chance,' said Dad.

I went upstairs to my bedroom with Pink Rabbit hopping along behind me and got out all my craft things for making the party invitations. I only had two more to make. Well, three if I was going to make one for Ava. I got busy with the scissors, cutting out cardboard rabbit shapes and sticking white pompoms on them to be the fluffy tails. Then I wrote the names of all my friends on the invitations along with the place and time of the party. I felt very pleased with how they all looked.

'Marvellous!' said Dad when I came downstairs a couple of hours later to show him.

'They're lovely!' said Mum. 'Do you want me to enchant them to bounce along like real rabbits with my wand?'

'Er . . . I don't think so,' I said. 'Last time I took enchanted invitations to school Miss Cherry wasn't very happy.' Instead, I gathered all the pink cardboard rabbits into a neat pile and slipped them into my satchel to take to school the following day.

Chapter TWO

Ava was already there when I arrived in the classroom the next morning. She was sitting at her desk with her hand placed protectively over the pocket of her dress, staring into space. When she saw me she quickly snatched her hand away from her pocket and folded her arms across her chest, glaring at me. I remembered what Dad had told me about giving Ava another

chance so I took a deep breath and walked towards her.

'Hi, Ava,' I said, forcing myself to smile. I reached into my satchel for her invitation.

'Hello,' said Ava, and I noticed her smirk as she caught sight of Pink Rabbit. I felt my cheeks get hot. 'What do you want?' she asked in the kind of voice that sounded like she didn't care. A voice that sounded like she thought she was so much more important and fantastic than anyone else. I stuffed the invitation back down into my satchel.

'It doesn't matter,' I squeaked, embarrassed and scurried back to my desk.

My face was still burning when Zoe walked into the classroom and sat down at the desk next to mine.

'I'm sorry I didn't bring my monkey, Coco!' she said. 'My mum wouldn't let me!'

'That's OK,' I said, feeling even more self-conscious now of Pink Rabbit sitting by my feet. Maybe I *was* too old to bring

a cuddly toy to school? Maybe Ava was right.

'Zoe!' I whispered. 'I've got something for you!' I reached into my satchel and pulled out her invitation.

'Ooh!' said Zoe as she read it. 'A teddy bears' picnic! For Pink Rabbit! At your house, this weekend!'

'Yes!' I whispered. 'Do you think you can come?'

'Definitely!' said Zoe. 'I can't wait! I'll make sure to bring Coco. Are you going to invite Ava?'

'I have to,' I said. 'I've got her invitation here. I'm going to give it to her later.'

'Well *I* don't think you should invite her,' said Zoe, defiantly. 'She'll only ruin it. She was so mean to us yesterday.'

'I know,' I said 'but don't you think—'

But then Miss Cherry put her hands up for silence in the classroom. She started

taking the register and there was no more
time to talk.

At break time, Zoe and I went around the
playground giving out the invitations to
the rest of our class.

'Cool!' said Bruno. 'I'll bring my toy
robot!'

'I'll bring my favourite cuddly
caterpillar!' said Sashi.

'Can I bring my mermaid doll?' asked
Samantha. 'Her hair changes colour in the
water!'

'Of course!' I replied as a new idea
popped into my head. 'I know! I'll ask my
Mum and Dad if we can get the paddling

pool out!'

'Yeah!' said Jasper excitedly. 'I'll bring
my swimming shorts!'

'Ooh! We could turn your slide into a
water slide!' added Zoe.

'YES!' squealed Sashi.

I beamed around at my friends. They
all seemed so enthusiastic about the party.

And no one was laughing at the idea of a teddy bears' picnic. It made me feel really happy, and much more confident about inviting Ava. I stared around the playground. Where was she? Her invitation was the last one in my bag.

'Oh, she asked Miss Cherry if she could stay in and read today,' Zoe said when I asked.

'Really!?' I asked disbelievingly.

Zoe shrugged and linked arms with me. Together we skipped towards the grass and the daisies. As we skipped I gazed around us at the bright blue sky and the sparkling sunshine. How could anyone want to stay inside on a day like this?

Ava was *obviously* avoiding us.

When we got back into the classroom after break time, Ava was sitting at her desk with her head down, busily scribbling in her notebook. I approached her nervously, my hand clutching the invitation tightly. I gave a polite cough.

Ava just ignored me and carried on writing with her arm curved around her notebook. She didn't look up. I felt a sting of annoyance. Who did she think she was? Coming into our classroom and being so . . . *horrible* and aloof!

'Just leave her,' whispered Zoe, tugging on my arm. 'Come on, Isadora!'

I let Zoe pull me away and then I stuffed the invitation deep down back into my satchel, not caring if it got crumpled.

Maybe Mum and Dad were wrong about inviting Ava to the party. It was so *obvious* that she would just spoil it. And I was so looking forward to my friends all coming over. It would be awful if Ava ruined the teddy bears' picnic. It was supposed to be Pink Rabbit's special day!

I wouldn't invite her, I decided. But for the rest of the morning I found it very hard to concentrate on my work. I couldn't stop thinking about the invitation, screwed up at the bottom of my satchel. The thought of not giving it to Ava made me feel so guilty.

I couldn't *really* not invite her, could I? I'd have to find another moment to give her the invitation.

Chapter THREE

That afternoon, Miss Cherry announced that we would be starting a new project.

'The name of our project is going to be Under the Sea!' she said.

'Ooh!' whispered the class and I felt my insides fizz with excitement. I love anything to do with the ocean, and I knew I would have a lot to say. I've had three magical underwater adventures with my mermaid friends.

'I'm going to split you all up into groups,' continued Miss Cherry. 'Zoe, can you go and sit with Sashi and Dominic, please? Samantha, you will be working with Oliver and Jasper. And Isadora, please will you go and sit with Ava and Bruno.'

I felt my heart sink like a stone.

Ava!

Suddenly I didn't feel very excited about the project at all. Reluctantly, I gathered up my things and went to sit at a table with Bruno and Ava. She didn't look very pleased to see us.

'We did this topic at my old school last year,' she said. 'It will be so boring to do it again!'

'Oh great!' said Bruno cheerfully. 'You can help us out then, Ava!'

'Hmph!' said Ava, and stuck her nose in the air.

Bruno looked at me, confused, and I looked back at him and shrugged.

'I'd like you all to start by writing down everything you know about the sea already,' said Miss Cherry, handing out sheets of paper. 'You can even draw pictures if you like!

36

Then we'll share our information with the rest of the class.'

Bruno grabbed his pen and immediately began doodling a picture of a starfish.

'I've got a good fact!' he said. 'Did you know that starfish have an eye on the end of each arm?'

Ava looked at Bruno scornfully.

'Don't be silly,' she said. 'Of *course* they don't!'

'They *do*!' Bruno insisted. 'We went to a sea life centre last summer and the guide there told us! If a starfish has five arms then it means it also has five eyes!'

'I don't believe you!' said Ava. 'That's

a stupid fact!'

Bruno looked hurt.

'I've got a fact about starfish too!' I said, remembering some of the amazing creatures I had seen on my underwater

adventure with Emerald the mermaid. 'Some starfish actually have *more* than five arms! I've seen one with at least twenty!'

'Cool!' said Bruno. 'It must have had twenty eyes then!'

I laughed, but Ava just scoffed.

'You're both making this rubbish up,' she said. 'Next I expect you'll tell me that mermaids are real.'

'They are!' I burst out before I could stop myself.

'Isadora's met one!' said Bruno.

Ava didn't reply straight away, but she stared at my vampire-fairy wings and my fangs.

'Well, I suppose you pretend to be

a magical creature yourself,' she said. 'It makes sense that you would say that other magical creatures exist. Where did you get your wings from? The costume shop?'

Bruno gasped.

I stared at Ava, my eyes filling with tears. Bruno looked very cross now.

'Isadora is a *real* vampire fairy!' he said. 'She has a magic wand and everything! Show Ava some magic, Isadora! Prove her wrong!'

I sniffed. I wasn't sure I felt like proving myself to Ava.

'Go on!' said Bruno, pushing my wand towards me.

I picked it up, my hands feeling all

clammy. Bruno stared at me expectantly,
his eyes sparkling. My friends love it
when I show them some magic, but today
I wasn't really in the mood. I felt flustered
and upset.

'Go on!' whispered Bruno
encouragingly.

I waved my wand, but my heart

wasn't in it.

Nothing happened.

Not even one tiny spark fizzled out
from the star on top.

'See!' crowed Ava. 'It's a fake wand
from a costume shop! I knew it!'

'Try again!' said Bruno. 'You can do it
Isadora!'

But I didn't want to try again.
Instead, I shook my head and put my

wand back down on
the table.

'I don't want to,'
I said. 'Not right now.
Let's get on with the
project.'

'Fine,' said Ava. 'But *I'm* going to work on my own. I can't trust anything you two say!'

Then she turned away from us both and busied herself with writing in her notebook. Bruno shuffled closer to me.

'We don't want to work with her

anyway!' he whispered crossly. 'Do we?'

I shook my head. Ava was mean, mean, *mean*!

There was *no* way I was going to invite her to Pink Rabbit's party now!

I was glad when the bell finally rang at the end of the school day. I couldn't wait to get out of the classroom and away from Ava. When I ran into the playground,

I saw Mum waiting for me with Honeyblossom in the pushchair. She was very busy chatting to Zoe's mum. They were discussing the teddy bears' picnic.

'I have a whole bag of leftover balloons from Zoe's last party,' Zoe's mum was saying. 'Would you like them, Cordelia?'

'Oh!' said Mum. 'That's *very* kind! But I was going to magic up some floating candyfloss clouds on strings instead! I've realized that balloons aren't terribly good for the environment you know. Nature is very important to fairies. The candyfloss clouds can be *eaten* afterwards!'

'How delicious!' said Zoe's mum.

'I'll make sure Zoe brings one home for you after the party!' Mum beamed. 'Oh hello, Isadora! You're looking a bit glum! Did you hand out all your party invitations?'

As Mum spoke I noticed Ava sidle past. She glanced at me and Zoe.

'Oh, uh . . .' I stuttered.

'Yes she did!' said Zoe loudly. 'Everyone who *should* have got an invitation to Pink Rabbit's party got one!'

'Oh good!' smiled Mum.

Ava stared at us and suddenly her face went very red. Her mouth turned down at the edges and she looked like she might be about to cry. Then she turned

away from us and ran off. I felt my throat tighten. Ava must have heard everything.

'Well!' said Mum brightly. 'We'd better be getting home. I thought we could stop in at the ice cream parlour on the way home, Isadora. It's such a lovely sunny day! They've got a new flavour called peaches and cream! I do so *love* peaches!'

Honeyblossom bounced up and down

excitedly in the pram.

I forced a smile, but I didn't really feel like eating ice cream. I held onto the side of the buggy and walked along the pavement with Mum. All I could think about was Ava's shocked, upset face.

'Are you all right?' asked Mum. 'You're very quiet this afternoon.'

'I'm fine,' I squeaked. For some reason, I couldn't bring myself to tell Mum about Ava and the invitation. I felt so guilty and so mean for not giving it to her, despite how horrid she had been to everyone.

Mum pushed open the door of the ice cream parlour and we stepped inside. A

rainbow of fruity flavours winked back at us. Mum ordered peaches and cream for all three of us and we sat on tall stools to eat them.

'Delicious!' said Mum as she spooned some into her mouth and then some into Honeyblossom's. 'Can you believe that such delicious things *just grow on trees*?! Well, not the ice cream of course, but the *peaches*! Wonderful!'

I shook my head as I swallowed. My ice cream tasted of cardboard.

Chapter
FOUR

As soon as I got home, I ran up to my bedroom with Pink Rabbit hopping along behind me and threw myself on my bed.

'What am I going to do?' I asked him. 'I've done something so horrible!'

Pink Rabbit patted my shoulder with his paw. I knew he was trying to tell me that it wasn't completely my fault. That

Ava *had* made it very difficult for me to give her the invitation. But still, I knew that I *should* have given it to her. It wasn't fair to leave her out when I had invited everyone else to the party. I felt terrible and I couldn't get the image of Ava's sad face out of my head.

After a while, there came a tip-tap of feet on the stairs and Dad popped his head round my bedroom door. He must have just woken up from his daily sleep. My dad is a vampire so he sleeps through the day.

'Isadora?' he asked. 'Can I come in? Mum tells me that you're a bit out of sorts.'

I sat up on my bed and nodded.

Dad came in and sat down next to me.
He smelt of hair gel and shoe polish.
Grooming is very important to vampires.

'What's the matter?' he asked. 'Why
don't you tell me or Mum? A problem

shared is a problem halved you know!'

'Is it?' I asked doubtfully.

'Well, let's try and see,' replied Dad.
'What's happened?'

I pulled my knees up to my chest and
suddenly the whole story came spilling
out of me. About how mean Ava had been.
About not finding the right moment to
give her the invitation and then deciding
to not give it to her at all. About her sad,
shocked face when she found out about the
party.

And she said that I wasn't even a real
vampire fairy!' I sniffed. 'She was really
horrid to everyone. But I still feel so bad
about not inviting her to the party!'

Dad wrapped me up in his big black vampire cape.

'It sounds like a *conundrum*,' he said. 'But you know there's only really one right thing to do . . .'

'I have to invite Ava,' I said.

'Yes,' said Dad.

'But it's going to be even more awkward to invite her *now*!' I said. 'After she knows that I didn't invite her in the first place!'

'Well, better late than never,' said Dad. 'You can give her the invitation first thing tomorrow.'

'It's a bit crumpled,' I said.

'I'll give it a little iron,' said Dad.

'Well . . . OK,' I agreed.

Even though the idea of giving the invitation to Ava the next day made me nervous, I felt a lot better after I told Dad everything, and once I had made a decision about what to do.

'Let's go for a fly before evening breakfast,' suggested Dad. 'It will clear your head.'

'OK!' I said, jumping up from the bed and suddenly feeling a lot more like my usual sparky self. I love it when Dad and I go for a fly. We hold hands and Dad can whizz really fast!

Dad opened the window and we leapt out into the late afternoon sky. The sun was still shining and everything looked like it had been sprinkled with gold dust.

We flew over the roads and trees, towards the park where I could see the duck pond twinkling in the light. My hair streamed out behind me as Dad whooshed us along and for those few moments, I forgot all

about Ava and the party. I was just a little vampire-fairy in a big blue sky, feeling the lovely warm breeze rush past my pointed ears.

'Look!' said Dad, pointing down at the pond. 'Ducklings!'

I stared down at the park below us. Swimming around in the pond were twelve tiny, fluffy ducklings. They were following the big mother duck in a line and pecking at the pondweed.

'Oh!' I cried. 'Let's go closer!'

Dad and I landed on the ground inside the park. As we walked towards the pond, I noticed that Dad and I weren't the only ones who had spotted the ducklings. There were three humans standing by the edge of the water watching them too.

Two grown-ups and a girl.

A girl who I recognized.

I gripped onto Dad's hand tightly.

It was Ava.

I pulled on Dad's arm.

'Let's go home!' I hissed.

'What?' said Dad. 'Why? I thought you wanted to see the ducklings!'

'I've changed my mind!' I said, pulling hard on Dad's arm, and dragging him behind a bush.

'What *is* going on?' asked Dad, confused.

'It's Ava!' I said, pointing through the leaves.

Ava was standing by the pond, but she wasn't even looking at the ducklings. She was just staring into space.

'She doesn't look very

happy,' observed Dad.

'I know,' I whispered, feeling my insides twist with guilt once again.

I saw Ava reach her hand into her pocket, taking out something small and soft. It looked like a squashy little doll with pink hair. I frowned, remembering the way Ava had protectively touched her pocket that morning.

'Ava said *I* was too old to bring a toy to school!' I whispered indignantly. 'But she's secretly got one too! In her pocket!'

Dad shrugged.

'Maybe she was embarrassed about it,' he said. 'I guess it goes to show that you don't really know her at all.'

I continued peering through the leaves of the bush. I watched as Ava tore a page out of her notebook and fashioned a little paper boat for the doll to bob about in on the pond but then Dad pulled me back.

'We mustn't hide here, spying,' he said. 'It's not right! Why don't you go and talk to her right now and invite her to the party!'

'What?!' I gasped.

'Go on . . .' said Dad gently.

'I can't!' I said. 'I don't have her invitation with me!'

'I don't think that really matters,' said Dad.

'But . . . but . . .' I began.

'It's up to you,' said Dad. 'But either way, we can't stay hiding behind this bush any longer!'

I felt my heart begin to pitter-patter in my chest. The idea of walking up to Ava right now made me really nervous. I was *sure* she wouldn't be pleased to see me. What if she said something mean?

Then the image of Ava's sad, shocked face floated into my head again.

I made up my mind.

I took a deep breath.

And I walked out from behind the bush.

Ava didn't notice me at first. She

was busy watching her paper boat. But as I got nearer to the pond she glanced up. Her face went red. She looked very embarrassed. I forced myself to smile at her. My biggest, sparkliest vampire fairy smile.

'Hi, Ava!' I said.

Ava didn't reply, but her parents turned to look at me. They both beamed.

'Ava!' they said. 'Is this a friend from

your new school?'

'Er . . .' said Ava. Hurriedly, she
snatched the pink-haired doll out from
the paper boat and stuffed it back into her
pocket.

'I'm Isadora,' I said. 'I'm in Ava's
class.'

'Oh, how lovely!' said Ava's mum.

'How wonderful that you're already
making friends!' said her dad.

Ava's parents both seemed so kind and friendly, but Ava just shuffled her feet awkwardly and stared at the ground.

'We'd just come out for an evening walk,' said Ava's dad.

'Ava wanted to take Pippi for a sail,' said her mum.

'*Muuuum*,' said Ava.

'Pippi goes *everywhere* with Ava,' said her mum. 'She's very special. I'm sure you've probably already seen her with Ava at school!'

'Oh um . . . no,' I said. 'But I'd really *like* to see her! I have a special toy too. He's called Pink Rabbit! He's at home right now. Napping!'

Ava's parents looked delighted.
Then they turned to Dad and introduced
themselves to him. They all started
chatting about boring grown-up stuff.

Ava finally looked up and caught my
eye.

'You'd *like* to see Pippi?' she asked.

'Of course,' I replied.

Ava reached her hand into her pocket and brought out the little doll. It was very small and very pretty with big sewn on eyelashes and a ruffly dress spotted all over with stars.

'She has lots more clothes at home,'
said Ava a bit shyly. 'I've made her a whole
wardrobe of them!'

'Oh, I love making tiny clothes!' I
replied. 'I make them for the dolls in my
dolls' house sometimes. And sometimes
for Pink Rabbit too, but he doesn't really
like wearing clothes.'

Ava giggled. It was the first time I
had heard her laugh.

'I like Pippi,' I said.

'*You do?*' said Ava. And her face broke
into a smile. She sounded very relieved.
'My friends at my old school used to laugh
at me for always carrying her around,'
she whispered. 'They said it was babyish.

That's why I was trying to keep her a secret this time.'

'Well, I don't think you should keep her a secret any more!' I said. '*I* think she's so magical! I love her spiky eyelashes and her glittery, starry dress! She looks like she has lots of adventures.'

'Oh, she does!' replied Ava. 'I write them all down in my special notebook! She's been to all sorts of places and done all sorts of things!'

Ava began to tell me all about Pippi's latest adventure. As she talked, her eyes began to sparkle and her voice sounded all excited. I could tell that she loved Pippi and that Pippi was a big part of Ava.

Maybe Ava had been hiding that big part of herself in order to try and fit in.

How she *thought* she should try and fit in.

'Don't tell anyone else about Pippi though, will you?' said Ava when she finally came to the end of the story. 'I don't want the rest of the class to know about her.'

'But she's so important to you!' I said.

'*Exactly!*' said Ava.

'I don't think anyone in our class will make fun of you for having Pippi,' I insisted. 'Why would they? And anyway, anyone who makes fun of you for just being yourself is not a real friend.'

'That's true,' said Ava. 'I hadn't thought of it that way before.'

'*I* was worried about not fitting in when I first joined the class,' I said. 'I don't think anyone had seen a vampire fairy before, but everyone was so kind to me! And I *am* a real vampire fairy by the way.'

Ava looked embarrassed.

'I know,' she whispered. 'I'm sorry I said you weren't. I was just finding it hard and scary being in a new school and I was worried no one would find me interesting. Especially you! With your wings and wand and magic, real-life pink rabbit!'

'Oh!' I said in surprise.

Neither of us said anything for a moment and then I remembered why I had come over in the first place.

'I have an invitation for you,' I said. 'For you and Pippi! I wanted to give it to you today, but I couldn't find the right moment. I'm sorry I didn't give it to you earlier. Do you want to come to Pink Rabbit's party? It's going to be a

teddy bears' picnic in my garden. It's this
weekend!'

'I'd love to come,' Ava replied, happily.
'Thank you, Isadora! I thought I was the
only one not invited!'

She grinned at me and I grinned back. And then Dad tapped me on the shoulder and said it was time to go.

'Evening breakfast will be getting cold!' he said.

Ava and her parents looked confused.

'We have two breakfasts every day,'
I explained. 'Because Dad sleeps through
the day and gets up in the evening.'

Ava's parents nodded, but they looked
a little bemused.

'Bye, Ava!' I said.

'See you tomorrow, Isadora!' said Ava.

Then Dad took my hand and we rose into the air, soaring up high over the park. As we flew, I saw Ava turn and walk away from the park with her parents following. Except she wasn't walking. She was *skipping*!

Chapter FIVE

It was the morning of Pink Rabbit's party and I bounded down the stairs excitedly to answer the door. Zoe stood on the step outside, along with Sashi and Oliver. I had asked some of my friends to come a little bit earlier to help me out with something.

The four of us ran up to my bedroom where the floor was strewn with paper and paint, glitter, and sequins.

'It's almost ready!' I said.

'It looks good!' said Zoe. 'Let me help you paint the last bits.'

'I'll put strings on it!' said Oliver.

We sat in silence for a while, concentrating hard on what we were doing, while Pink Rabbit and Coco the monkey bounced on the bed. (Coco used to be Zoe's favourite stuffed toy, but I magicked her alive for Zoe one time during a sleepover.)

'It's done!' said Zoe, standing back to admire her handiwork.

'It's so sparkly!' said Oliver.

'It's perfect!' I said.

Together we carried our creation
back down the stairs and Mum
and Dad helped to hang it
up in the hallway.

'How thoughtful of you all!' said Mum.

'It was Isadora's idea,' said Zoe.

'I know it's Pink Rabbit's party, but I just want Ava to feel *really* welcome!' I said.

Hung all the way across the grand entrance hall of our house was a huge, colourful banner, sprinkled all over with glitter and sequins. Written in big letters all the way across it were the words:

Welcome Ava and Pippi

We were all standing in the hallway admiring the banner when the doorbell rang.

'Another guest!' said Mum. 'I'll go and lay the picnic rug out.'

'I'd better prepare the red jelly!' said Dad.

I opened the door.

Ava stood on the step. She looked a little nervous. Clutched in her hand was Pippi, wearing a tiny paper party hat and a very fancy dress.

'Hello, Isadora,' said Ava. 'Hello, Pink Rabbit!' Then she looked up and saw the banner hung across the hallway. She went

92

silent for a moment and her eyes became
very big and round.

'Is that for *me*?' she squeaked.

I nodded.

'It's your welcome party too, today!'
I told her. 'Pink Rabbit said he didn't
mind sharing.'

Pink Rabbit
wiggled his ears to
show he agreed.

Ava smiled. A
big, surprised, happy
smile. And then she
leapt towards me
and gave me a
huge hug.

'Thank you!' she cried. 'This is already the nicest party I've ever been to and it hasn't even started yet!'

It wasn't long before the rest of the guests arrived. They all marvelled at the banner in the hallway, and then I took them outside into the garden where a picnic rug had been set up on the grass, along with a smaller picnic rug for all the toys. Mum had made a big, beautiful cake topped with shiny cherries, each in a whirl of whipped cream. There were sandwiches and crisps, slices of pizza and bowls of jelly, ice cream and sprinkles. We all gobbled the food and I glanced over to make sure that Ava was OK.

She was smiling and laughing, deep in conversation with Samantha who had brought her mermaid doll to the party.

Then, after the picnic, came the best part. As a treat, Mum said she would magic everyone's toys to life, just for a few hours. My friends squealed and gasped with delight as Mum whirled her

wand and sparks began to fizz and fly. My friends' toys sprang to life and began to run around the garden, chasing each other and having fun. I saw Ava dance with joy when Pippi began twirling and prancing through the daisies, picking one and using it as a little sun umbrella.

After that, Dad filled the paddling pool with water and we all changed into our swimming costumes and jumped in—except for Bruno's robot who was forbidden from going in the water.

'You'll go rusty!' Bruno told him.

Mum brought the slide over so that we could whoosh down it and go SPLASH into the pool. A little while later, when

everyone was dry, Mum lassoed a cloud down from the sky and tethered it to the ground to make a bouncy castle.

'Are you having a good time?' I asked Ava as I held her hand and we bounced up and down on the soft, fluffy cloud.

'The best time!' grinned Ava. 'I'm sorry I was ever so mean to you, Isadora!'

'I'm sorry I didn't give you more of a chance!' I said.

We both smiled at each other as we
soared up into the golden sunshiny sky.
Friends.

Turn the page
for some
Isadorable
things to make
and do!

How to make invitations

If you want to host a teddy bears' picnic,
just like Isadora, here's how to make some invitations!

What you will need:

★ Coloured paper

★ Scissors

★ Coloured pens or pencils

★ An adult to help you

Before you hand out your invitations, make sure your grown-up knows about your plans.

Method:

1. Decide what shape you would like your invitations to be. Isadora made hers in the shape of Pink Rabbit.

2. Cut your coloured paper into the shape you have chosen. Your helpful adult may come in handy at this point!

3. Make sure you include all the right information. Your guest will need to know:

   WHAT the invitation is for. Is it a teddy bears' picnic like Isadora's, or a birthday party, or something else?

   WHEN it is. Make sure you include the date and time.

   WHERE it is. You want your guests to go to the right place!

4. Give out your invitations!

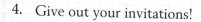

Which toy at the teddy bears' picnic would you most like to play with?

Take the quiz to find out!

What do you like to do for fun?

A. Crafting

B. Playing in the garden.

C. Constructing things with building blocks.

What are your favourite kinds of story?

A. Exciting adventure stories.

B. Stories about friendships.

C. Stories that have dramatic battles!

What do you like to do on a rainy day?

A. Get as wet as possible splashing in puddles.

B. Go outside, as long as I'm under an umbrella.

C. Stay inside, I do not like getting wet at all.

Results

Mostly As
You would like Ava's doll, Pippi! You'd love to make things for Pippi to play with and wear and make up fun adventures for her to go on!

Mostly Bs
You would like Isadora's very own Pink Rabbit! You're interested in other people, and love playing outside with your friends.

Mostly Cs
You would like Bruno's robot! You love building things, and hate getting wet—you don't want the robot to go rusty!

ISADORA·MOON

Goes to School

Half vampire, half fairy, totally unique!
Harriet Muncaster

Goes Camping

Half vampire, half fairy, totally unique!
Harriet Muncaster

Has a Birthday

Half vampire, half fairy, totally unique!
Harriet Muncaster

Goes to the Ballet

Half vampire, half fairy, totally unique!
Harriet Muncaster

Gets in Trouble

Half vampire, half fairy, totally unique!
Harriet Muncaster

Goes on a School Trip

Half vampire, half fairy, totally unique!
Harriet Muncaster

Goes to the Fair

Half vampire, half fairy, totally unique!
Harriet Muncaster

Makes Winter Magic

Half vampire, half fairy, totally unique!
Harriet Muncaster

MIRABELLE

Meet Isadora's naughty cousin,
Mirabelle Starspell, in her very own stories.

From the world of ISADORA MOON

MIRABELLE
Gets up to Mischief

Half witch, half fairy, totally naughty!
Harriet Muncaster

From the world of ISADORA MOON

MIRABELLE
Breaks the Rules

Half witch, half fairy, totally naughty!
Harriet Muncaster

From the world of ISADORA MOON

MIRABELLE
Has a Bad Day

Half witch, half fairy, totally naughty!

Harriet Muncaster

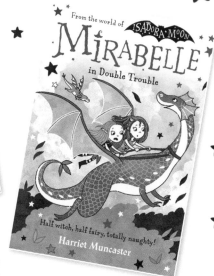

From the world of ISADORA MOON

MIRABELLE
in Double Trouble

Half witch, half fairy, totally naughty!

Harriet Muncaster

From the world of ISADORA MOON

MIRABELLE
and the Naughty Bat Kittens

Half witch, half fairy, totally naughty!

Harriet Muncaster

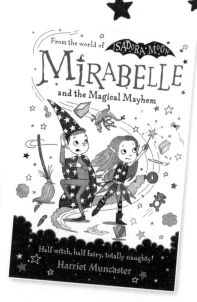

From the world of ISADORA MOON

MIRABELLE
and the Magical Mayhem

Half witch, half fairy, totally naughty!

Harriet Muncaster

Get ready to meet Isadora's mermaid friend, Emerald!

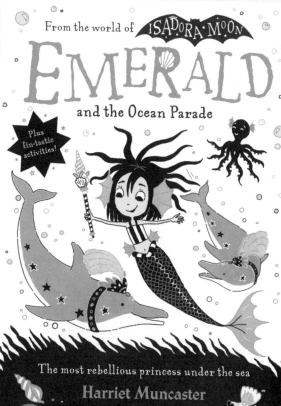

From the world of ISADORA MOON

EMERALD
and the Ocean Parade

Plus fin-tastic activities!

The most rebellious princess under the sea

Harriet Muncaster

Harriet Muncaster, that's me! I'm the
author and illustrator of Isadora Moon.
Yes really! I love anything teeny tiny,
anything starry, and everything glittery.

For information on the
Isadora Moon animation,
check out the instagram page

@isadoramoon

To visit Harriet Muncaster's website, visit
harrietmuncaster.co.uk

Love Isadora Moon?
Why not try these too...